# Sugah

# Sugah

Lilly Buchanan

Published by Lilly Buchanan, 2024.

SUGAH

**First edition. February 26, 2024.**

Copyright © 2024 Lilly Buchanan.

ISBN: 979-8224646135

Written by Lilly Buchanan.

# Lilly Buchanan

LILLY
BUCHANAN
SUGAH

1962

A girl named Sugah
Lilly Buchanan, Author


This story's characters are not in the likeness of anyone living or dead.
This is strictly a fiction story from the imagination of the author.

**To my baby brother Mark Thomas. I love you Pookie and I believe in you!!**

Sugah was born Melba Willie Pearl Nugent, in Escanaba, Mississippi in June of 1962 Escanaba was a small town, with a population of 215. It was 217, but Mr. Hertz died and then Sugah's sister Jana ran away, making it 215. Sugah had a hobby of keeping score of the coming and going of residents.

Everybody knew everybody in that country town. Country bars were filled on Fridays and Saturdays and country churches were filled on Sundays.

If you didn't know what you were doing, your neighbors surely did. Angela Downey was famous for saying, "If you want to have an affair, you better rent a car in Mobile and travel 50 miles from there, in the opposite direction of here, and in disguise, or everyone will know."

Our girl Sugah was 12 years old, childlike forever in her mind, however, almost everyone accepted her and some even adored her. Arlene, Sugah's mama took her shopping with her when she went. 2 stores were not friendly to Sugah. One was Winnie's. It was filled with beautiful crystal glass and fineries. Sugah had accidentally knocked over an expensive biscuit basket and the salesperson yelled at her and told her to, " get out and don't come back".

Sugah couldn't understand why her mama went there once a month. She waited patiently on the steps for her mama to come out. It kind of made her mad that her Mama would go into a shop she was not welcomed into. She never knew her mama was making monthly payments to pay off the crystal glass Sugah had accidentally broken. The owner had called the Pastor then he went to see Arlene to tell her what happened. Arlene went and spoke to the owner, asking her to forgive Sugah, and asking to make payments on the broken glass.

The next store was Michaelson Hardware Store. Sugah was deeply impressed by that store. It had hundreds of different things in it. The owner said it wasn't proper for a young girl to hang around a hardware store, so he told her Mama to keep her out of there unless she was buying something. That made Sugah cry. She didn't understand how people could be so mean.

Sugah was a sweetheart, she would visit you, pick flowers out of your prize garden, and hand them to you when you opened the door. Much to your dismay, though like a good Christian, you smiled and ooo'd and awed at the lovely bouquet.

Her mama, Arlene, went into labor with Sugah when her own doctor had fallen ill. A new young doctor was called in to deliver. Sugah was stuck inside her mama. After many hours of horrible labor, the doctor used something called forceps to pull Sugah from her mama's body. Sugah was stuck inside her mother, her head behind the pelvic bone. The new doctor used too much force and it greatly disfigured Sugah's head and also caused injury to her brain. She would forever be young, slow, and sweet.

Sugah was the last of 5 children, she had one sister, Jana, and the other 3 were boys. When Sugar was 4 years old, her Daddy was coming home from work, after working a double shift at the paper mill, the next town over. The security rails of the train did not lower, and the train hit him on the driver's side, killing him instantly. He never stood a chance. The doctors swore he died instantly and did not suffer.

His coworkers and friends paid for his funeral. There was a little money left over and they had their wives give the money to Arlene to help with the children.

Arlene took in laundry, cleaned houses, sold plants in the spring, made and sold homemade preserves, grew and sold vegetables... anything to provide for her family.

Her 3 sons cut grass and did odd jobs around town to help the family. The boys were very athletic like their daddy. They were the pride of their high school and eventually would go to colleges on 100% scholarships.

Sugah was not one for school. She stayed until the 6th grade but she would get bored and leave and go home without asking anyone. Arlene and the principal agreed it would be best to keep Sugah home. Of course,

Sugah never stayed home for long, she loved to ramble around the town. Exploring the town, the people, and the land.

Mr. Glass the owner of the general store would allow her to take the fruit that was not quite bad, but not good enough to sell with a good conscience. Sugah loved that because it meant fried pies or cobblers would be made by her mama. Mr. Glass also let Sugah pick a candy each time she came. He would tell her, "If you give me a smile then that is my gift to you Sugah." She would say thank you. Then a huge smile would cross her face. Sometimes people would hand Sugah a penny. If that happened, she would run to the general store and say to Mr. Glass, "This is my gift to you." She never begged. People just knew she came from a poor family and felt sorry for her.

As hard as Arlene worked, she was unable to keep up with the payments on the house. Her church approached her with a solution. They would take over the payments and all she had to do was clean the church twice a week, the boys had to cut the grass.

It was 5 years later when the paper mill union's lawyer got the insurance from the train to pay for the accidental injury or death of Arlene's husband. At the insistence of every worker, Sugah's daddy's death resulted in a huge check for the family.

Arlene began to receive a monthly check, which allowed her to start making her house payment and there was a little left over to live on. She was able to cut back on a few of her jobs, giving her more time to keep up with Sugah.

Sugah was fine being alone. Her brothers had abandoned them for college and never looked back. Being around people made her feel nervous.

Other than her daily trip to the store, she preferred to be alone. She wasn't very smart but she knew very quickly when people didn't like her. Just like an animal knows when it's not wanted, Sugah could tell.

It was her job to collect the eggs. Her mama had taught her to be very careful because the eggs were very fragile. One Saturday, Sugah went to collect the eggs. She saw someone had left the pen open and the chickens were gone. They left 15 eggs in their boxes. Sugar carefully put them in her bowl and took them to her mama. By the time she got to her mama, she was crying.

"Sugah! What's wrong darling?"

"Somebody, somebody didn't close the pen. All our chickens is gone."

Her mama hugged her and said, "Now don't you worry bout some runaway chickens. They always come back home to eat."

Sugah tried to calm down, but this was very stressful for her.

"Mama, I think I need to lay down so I can calm down. I love them chickens."

"My sweet baby, I agree with you. Go rest. Everything will be fine."

Once Sugah left the room, Arlene grabbed the telephone and started calling her neighbors. Within 2 hours, those renegade chickens were back in their coop.

After Sugah woke up from her nap, her mama said, "Baby go make sure the coop is locked."

"But Mama, they all ran away."

"Just do as I say Sugah," Arlene said, both cool and calm.

Sugah went outside and her mama heard her shouting, "Oh thank you, Jesus! Mama our

chickens is back. I locked the pen real good mama. I am so happy."

She ran back in and gave her mama a big hug. Mama said, "See? We just need to have faith that

the good Lord is going to work things out."

Sugah's eyes got wide and she said, "He did Mama. He worked it all out and brought them

chickens back too!"

Arlene laughed and mussed Sugah's hair. She loved her daughter so much and was so grateful

to have her in her life. Even if she was a little different, Arlene wouldn't take cash money for

having Sugah. She was such a blessing to Arlene and most of the community. Those who

didn't like her just didn't understand Sugah.

It was time for Sugah's annual physical. Sugah begged her mama to go in with her.

Arlene said, "You are a big girl now."

Sugah stubbornly folded her arms and said, "I am not going unless you go in with me."

Arlene gave in and said, "Okay, Okay, I will go in with you."

The nurse told them that Doctor Pete had retired and they would be seeing a new

doctor, Dr. Ramsey.

Docter Ramsey dismissed Arlene by saying, "Ma'am you can wait outside."

Sugah said, "Oh no she aint.. If she goes, I'm going too."

The doctor just sighed. He began his physical. Everything checked out well.

He looked at Arlene and said, "What's wrong with her?"

Arlene became upset and said, "Perhaps you should read the files on the patients

to keep you from making a jackass of yourself."

He sighed again, then asked Sugah, "Sugar are you sexually active?".

Arlene screamed, "No she is not, and I don't appreciate you asking. Come on Sugah, we are

leaving."

All the way home, Arlene heard, "What sexually active mean mama?"

" Honey I will 'splain it to you after dinner."

They walked without talking the rest of the way home. Arlene was praying Sugah

would just forget about it. But of course, she did not.

Sugah asked Arlene, "Mama can I help with the dishes tonight?"

Arlene said, "Well, of course, you can Sugah, thank you for the help."

Sugah cleared the table as Arlene sipped on her sweet tea, silently praying Sugah

had forgotten the conversation with the doctor. Arlene heard the dishwater

running into the basin, so she got up to make sure the water wasn't too hot.

Sugah smiled and said, "Mama you always there when I need to learn something."

Arlene smiled and said, "That's what God gave you a mama, to show you the way. You weren't

born knowin' how to fetch eggs, wash dishes, or even make your bed. I showed you and I am

happy to keep showing you things. You are a good learner baby."

After the dishes were washed and put away, Sugah took a bath, kissed her mama, and went to

bed.

Arlene felt peaceful and relieved for about 5 minutes, she picked up her Bible and then there was a knock on the door.

Population 216 ½

Arlene called out, "Whose there?"

Her daughter Jana spoke up, "It's me, mama. I need to come home."

Arlene jerked the door open and held it for Jana to come in. They hugged each

other for what seemed like a long time. Jana had been gone a year and a half. She

never called nor sent a letter but her mama never stopped praying for her to come home.

When Arlene let go of her, she saw the baby bump.

"How far along are you honey?"

"I'm 4 months I think."

" Well sweet girl sit down and rest. Do you want tea or lemonade?"

"Your tea would really hit the spot mama."

Arlene went to the kitchen and brought her a plate from dinner and a large glass

of tea.

"Oh, my goodness mama I sure have missed your cooking!" Jana said as she

scarfed the food down.

Arlene realized Jana looked hollow and dirty. Jana ate like she hadn't eaten in a week.

"Jana, I have some peach pies left over from dinner, would you like 2 of those?"

Jana blushed and said, "Just bring me one mama, and some more tea."

They cried a little bit, then laughed and talked about who was still in town.

Arlene gave her a little gossip about the town and she and Jana laughed about it.

Finally, Arlene got up and said, "Let me take your things to your bedroom. You

know where the bathroom is, you just remember this is your home. Let me know

if you need anything. I love you Jana Michele and I sure thank God to see your

pretty face."

Jana hugged and kissed her mama and began to cry. "Mama, I have missed y'all so

much. I haven't got much clothes with me, Mama. After my bath, can we sleep with you?"

Arlene said, "Of course you can baby."

While Jana was taking her bath, Arlene put the suitcase in Jana's bedroom, then

she went to her own room and brought out one of her nightgowns and a pair

of house shoes for Jana to wear. She knocked at the bathroom door and Jana was

bathing, "Sweetheart, I'm going to lay these on the table here for you to put on

after your bath."

Jana smiled and said, "Thank you, mama."

When Arlene stepped out of the bathroom, she had to hold her breath. There was

a terrible stench coming from the bathroom. There was no telling the last time Jana had a proper

bath. All sorts of things ran through her mind. "Was Jana on the run from someone? Was she

homeless? Did the baby's father run out on her?"

Tears welled up in Arlene's eyes but she decided she was not going to bring it up until lunch the

next day. That would give Jana time to rest.

Arlene gave the bathroom a good scrub down with bleach and Pine-Sol after Jana went to sleep.

Jana slept until the next afternoon. That was good because it gave Arlene time to

explain to Sugah that her sister was back home.

"Sugah do not be asking Jana any questions. When she is ready, she will tell us

what happened. Ya hear?"

Sugah said, "Yes ma'am."

Arlene had to wake Jana up to eat. "Baby, I am sorry to bother you but supper is ready and you two need to eat to keep up your strength."

"Yes ma'am. I just need to wash my face and I will be in there."

Arlene made all of her favorites. Meatloaf, mashed potatoes, black-eyed peas,

corn on the cob, and cornbread. The dessert was a blackberry cobbler.

Jana hugged Sugah, then hugged her mama. Jana started to cry but her mama

stopped her. "Sweetheart it's okay if you cry, that there is your hormones. Now

wipe those tears and come eat."

Jana smiled and said, "Yes ma'am. "When she came into the dining room she gasped,

"Oh, mama, you have prepared a feast."

Sugah was unusually quiet but she asked, "What's a hormone?"

Arlene smiled and said, "Hush Sugah. Now, the vegetables were a gift from the

neighbors, they love to farm and give us some of what they grow. I have a freezer

full. Sugah provided the eggs because she collects them every day for us"

Sugah whispered, "Well I didn't lay the dang things. I just pick em up."

"Mama that is so wonderful. I can help you with any chores you have. Sugah why

you so quiet?" Jana said.

Sugah smiled and said, "Mama told me don't be asking you no questions and I got

nothing but questions so I am hushed."

Mama winced, then said, "Come on my girls we can talk later."

Arlene blessed the food and they ate abundantly.

Those girls ate so much, their mama was scared they might burst.

Afterward, Jana said, "Mama can I go back to bed?"

Arlene said, "Sure you can honey." Then she turned to Sugah and said, "Come on

Sugah help me with these dishes."

Sugah stared at Jana and shrugged her shoulders. Later, Arlene went into her bedroom

and looked at Jana's feet, they were swollen. She put 2 pillows under Jana's feet.

"Jana honey try to rest with your feet up, it will help the swelling go down.'"

Jana said, "Yes ma'am. Is it normal for your feet to swell up like this?"

Arlene said, "Yes baby sometimes it is. You just need rest and your family's love. It's gonna be

all right." Arlene rubbed Jana's back until she fell asleep. Jana fell asleep on her full stomach.

Arlene was praying over her and spoke kindly to her...

"Oh, my precious Jana Michelle, I have missed you so much. I am so thankful God brought you

back home. I don't care under what circumstance. I love you. Sleep good my girl. You are home,

you are safe and we will get through this together."


Sugah was making a lot of noise in the kitchen, trying to get her mama's attention.

Arlene came into the kitchen and said, "What is all this noise about Sugah?"

Sugah shrugged her shoulders and said, "I don't know mama. You told me

not to ask sister any questions. Is she dying?"

Arlene took the rag out of her hand and said, "Sit down baby, let's talk."

They sat down at the kitchen table. Arlene poured them both a cold glass of
water.

"Sweetheart, remember when we went to the doctor the other day and he asked
if you were sexually active?"

Sugah nodded her head yes.

"Well, it upset me because I wasn't ready for him to ask you that. You and me
hadn't had the talk we bout to have now." Arlene cleared her throat. She was nervous. She
didn't want to scare Sugah but it had to be done.

"See when a grown man and a grown woman love each other, they get married and they have
sexual relations. Some people shorten it by calling it having sex. Now let's see...the part that
you pee-pee out of is different from men. A man's part that he pee-pees out of, and
a woman's part that she pees out of, well they are different. These are the parts that married
people use to make a baby. They touch each other and that makes a baby. That is called sexual
relations."

"Well, why the heck would that doctor ask me that question then?" Sugah said with her eyes
bugged out, her face contorted with disgust.

Sugah's response caught Arlene by surprise and she bowed her head and pressed her lips together
to keep from laughing.

"Well sweetheart, there some girls that do go around having sex before they married. Most of the time, they think they are in love, and then the boy just

drops them like a bad habit. The boy may make all kinds of promises, then disappear if they

make a baby. Leaving the girl to usually be in trouble with their families."

Sugah was quiet for a moment then said, "Since we having a talk, mama. Is Jana

having a baby? Was she sexually active? Was she married?"

"Yes, she is gonna have a baby, but I don't know if she is married, sweetheart. She is not

ready to talk. I will let you know when I find out."

Sugah nodded her head and got up to finish the dishes.

As Arlene tucked Sugah in for the night, Sugah asked, "What we gone do with a baby Mama?"

"We gonna love it and help it be happy. You will be a big help with the baby Sugah."

Sugah sighed and said, "I don't know. I guess I can teach it to get the eggs and fish."

Arlene laughed and said, "Now that sounds like a big plan for when its gets older."

Sugah was satisfied with her mama's answer.

They said Sugah's nighttime prayers and it wasn't long before Sugah was snoozing.

Afterward, Arlene sat on the porch, drinking coffee, and reading her

Bible. She heard a noise, like a racing car. She looked up to see a beat-up old truck pull up fast

into her yard. A man got out. He runs up to the porch. He must have worked on cars or

something because he was filthy. He had drawings all over his arms, and earrings. He

barked loudly, "Jana here?"

Arlene stood up and said, "No I haven't seen my daughter in over a year and a

half. Who are you? Do you know where she might be?"

He smiled a big grin and said, "My name is Doctor Feel Good. I'm her old man. You tell her if

she shows up here, I'm looking for her. It's time for baby to come home."

Arlene's heart was racing. She felt the spirit of David rise up in her as she confronted this

Goliath. She stood up and marched right up to the large man. With her

Bible in her hand, she said, "I rebuke you in the name of Jesus Christ. I pray you

never find her, even if it means I never see her again."

The man looked shocked and ran back to his truck, squealing his tires as he left.

Arlene walked back inside her home and realized Jana was standing behind the door.

Jana burst into tears and Arlene held her until she quit crying.

"Thank you, mama. You saved my life and you don't even know it. He would have beat

me up and probably killed the baby. Thank you, Mama."

They sat down in the living room. Jana said, "Mama, what I am about to tell you is terrible

and I hope you don't hold it against me. I was tricked. I answered an ad in the paper for

young people to tell magazine subscriptions.

They said we would see the world and have great adventures. They promised a lot of money.

They talked about climbing the ladder of success and becoming managers. They said managers would get a new car and money for a new wardrobe every year. They made it sound so

glamorous. I was happy to have a job, to move away from here, and make something out of

myself. Amanda and I had talked about it and I decided I would go first, then send for her

once I was making a great living so I could help her get started. But it turned out to be evil. They

were cruel. If we didn't sell any magazines, they would slap up around, and once we started to

sell, if we didn't sell a certain amount of magazines, they wouldn't let us eat. They would get

food and eat it right in front of us. It was the cruelest thing I have ever seen. We didn't have a

shower and they made us use the bathrooms in buckets. It was so awful. We were living in

storage sheds. We would bathe off in gas station bathrooms about once a week.

They always made another person stay with us as we went door to door to try and sell these

Magazines so we could not escape or ask for help. It was a couple of months before I escaped by

running into a café.

I asked them to call the sheriff. They did, he took me to the place they were holding us and it was locked up. He had someone break the lock and it was filled with bunk beds, water buckets, and pee buckets, but they had cleared out fast. The deputy gave me 20 bucks and took me back to the café to eat. The owner was looking for a waitress so I asked if I could be his waitress. I guess he felt sorry for me. He had a room in the back of the café, with a bunk and a shower. I thought it would be safe since the bad people had cleared out. It turns out I was pretty good at waitressing, people liked me and tipped me real good. I was able to buy some clothes and shoes. I needed them so bad; those magazine evil people took all of my stuff.

One day it was kinda of slow and a man in a suit came in and had a piece of pie and coffee. He was clean-shaven and smelled good. His suit looked new. We did a little small talk as I wiped all the tables and the countertops. He asked if I would give him my telephone number.

I told him no because I didn't have a telephone number. He said, "I would really like to take you to a nice dinner. I'm not married, no kids. I work for a company that sells houses. Just think about it and give me a call." He left his business card with a large tip.

He came in 3 more times and left big tips. I would watch him drive away in a new car and wonder if my luck had changed, before I finally gave him a call. He took me to a very nice restaurant but he didn't talk to me much. We kind of ate in silence. I tried to make small talk but he didn't seem interested. I just figured he didn't like me after all. He drove me back towards the café where I was staying but then he took a left turn instead of a right turn. When I asked him why he didn't turn on the road to the café, he said he had to make a stop. We seemed to drive in circles. I told him to just let me out I would take a cab home. He said, "No I found the place." It was another storage shed, I was really scared by then. We stopped and he came to my side and opened the door. He dragged me out of the car by my hair and when we got to the storage door, he banged on it real hard and someone opened the door. It was the guy who came here just a little bit ago. The man in the storage shed looked me over and handed the guy some money. I was shaking all over. He tied my hands together and yelled at me to sit down. It was dark in there, then I saw 6 other girls sitting down on the far wall. They were all sitting up but asleep. He pushed 3 pills into my mouth and gave me some water. I hid the pills in my mouth, then spit them out when he turned away. There was a crack in the wall that I put the pills in when he wasn't watching. Throughout the night 10 other girls were brought by the man who was dressed in the suit.

I prayed so hard cause I didn't know what they were gonna do with us. I think it was like 2 nights later, the man in the suit came and brought us something to eat, then gave us fancy dresses to put on. He gave us high heels to wear and perfume. Another car came and took 5 girls out. A second car came and took the other 5 out. I asked, "What is gone happen to me? The dirty man said, 'You pretty girl, gone by my old lady.'

I asked, "What does that mean?"

He laughed and said, "You are my property. You are mine."

I asked, "What is happening to the other girls?

He said, "Them working girls. They gonna make us some money."

I didn't understand, so he got real close to my face and said, 'You ever had sex with a real man?'

I told him," I ain't never had sex with an unreal man. And I don't intend to until I'm married."He laughed. Then he shook me hard and slapped me 3 or 4 times. He gave me different clothes to put on. Like a tee shirt and some pants.

I think it was 2 days later, a strange man came in and said he was a preacher. I got mad and said to the dirty man, "I don't know you; how can I marry you?"

He smiled and said, "Just shut up and listen to the nice preacher."

In 3 minutes, the preacher proclaimed us married. I don't think it was legal. The preacher smelled awful and was falling over. I don't think he was a preacher at all. The dirty man kept calling me his old lady. He never told me his real name. He drove me to a house. I don't know how far away but it seemed like a hundred miles. There were so many many dogs.

"When I got out of his truck, he said," Welcome home, honey. When you need something from town let me know. Keep my dogs fed and watered."

"I was hysterically crying and pushing him away. He finally got tired of hitting me and he let me sleep in my own room until I calmed down. I accepted what was happening to me. It was my own fault for leaving town. It must have been about 4 months ago. I had cooked dinner like you taught me and then cleaned the house. I had decorated it to look like a normal home. He came in, smiled then, and then dragged me by my hair, up to one of the rooms. He said," It's time. You got me out here sleeping with these working girls, but I ain't married to them. He tore my dress off..." Jana started sobbing and her mother held her.

"It's okay baby. You are home now. It will be okay you are safe."Arlene took Jana to a doctor's appointment in Freedom County which was about 40 away from Escanaba. The baby was healthy and the doctor put Jana on prenatal vitamins. Jana was fortunate to not have any diseases.

"Do you want to put the baby up for adoption Jana?" the doctor asked.

Jana looked at her mama but didn't answer. She hung her head down and began to cry.

Arlene said," No we are going to keep it and I will help her raise it." Jana sobbed with relief. Once they got home, Jana confessed to her mother. "I feel like there is a demon in me because it came from the dirty man. I am so ashamed mama. I couldn't stop it. He hurt me over and over, it was awful. What will this baby be like? Will it be like me? Or him? I'm scared Mama." Arlene held her and told her, "Jana Michelle NOBODY comes in this world without God's Permission. He tells us in his word that He knew us before we were born and woven together in our mother's womb. Don't you be sad or ashamed. You were hurt by those people but God Himself spared your life and this child's life."

"But what if I can't love it, Mama?"

"Then I will love the baby for you, Jana. I did a pretty good job with you and Sugah and the

3 boys. It won't bother me one bit to raise that baby as my own because you see that's my

grandchild Jana. And I could never let you give it away to strangers. Honey, I love you and I am here to help you. Whatever you decide to do with your life, work? Go to school? I will support

you and God will support us."

Jana sobbed again, but this time was with happiness.

Arlene had asked the Pastor if he could counsel Jana or, did he think she needed a different type

of therapy. He suggested a woman doctor in a town over. The woman was familiar with

people who had been victimized. For the next 4 months, Arlene took Jana to the doctor once a

week. The doctor was very good at what she did and she helped Jana deal with a lot of the guilt

and trauma that she had been through. She also wanted Jana to tell the police everything that had

happened so they might look for these awful people. This scared the death out of Jana.

Jana begged her, "Please don't make me. They will come and kill my family. Please can't I

just wait until I give birth and get back on my feet?"

The doctor tried to calm her down. "Jana you are safe with your mother. I still have to report

this to the police because you are a victim. But you can wait until you give birth to go and

give your statement. You must believe you are safe, Jana."

"Yes, ma'am. I'm just so scared still. Girls disappeared that were not making enough money

I don't know if they killed them or sent them to another city. I remember the dirty man

threatening them, "If you think I'm bad, wait until you meet my partner Rico. He has an electric

cow prod that he will zap you with if you don't make enough money. I'm giving you cows every chance to make the money, it's up to you. All I can do is put you out there, the rest is up to you.

In 3 months if you haven't made enough money, you get a free ride to Rico. Not many girls make

it out of Rico's place. The burns are just too painful to go on living with. One girl ran in front of

a semi-truck to get away from Rico, and another jumped off a building. Life is tough with Rico."

I watched in horror as the ones that were being traded out collapsed and begged not to be sent

away. The dirty man shot them up with some drugs and the women were carried out."

Jana went into labor, and Arlene rented them a motel room near the hospital in Freedom.

On the third night, Arlene, Sugah, and Jana went to the hospital. Jana was in a lot of pain. She

screamed, "Mama this hurts so bad. Is this normal? Is something wrong?"

Arlene held her hand and tried to comfort her. "This soon will pass my sweet daughter. The

baby will be a great reward for this suffering."

Sugah was terrified, she said, "I ain't nevah having a baby if it hurts this bad Mama."

Arlene smiled bravely, and Sugah said nothing. She was too busy praying for Jana.

"Is she gone die, Mama? I nevah seen Jana hurt so bad. I am so scared for her."

Arlene hugged Sugah and said, "It hurts for the baby to come out, but later she will forget

all the pain of having a baby after she heals."

Sugah looked around the maternity waiting room. "Mama who are all these men?

Are they waiting on Jana's baby to be born?"

Arlene calmly said, "No Sugah. Their wives are also having babies. They are waiting

patiently like we are to see the babies when they are born."

Jana was finally reeled into the delivery room. She cried out to her mother but the staff would not

allow Arlene to be in the delivery room. They made Arlene and Sugah continue to wait outside

in the waiting room.

In just about 25 minutes, the nurse came outside, holding the baby to show the

family. She was beautiful. Arlene cried.

"Is Jana, okay?" she asked the nurse.

"Yes, ma'am she did just fine. We gave her something to sleep. She was pretty upset."

It was several hours before they could see the new mama.

Arlene took Sugah to the cafeteria in the hospital. Sugah was amazed. "Mama, I never been to a

hospital. I can't believe they have a restaurant inside a hospital."

Arlene smiled and said, "Well all the people that work here have to eat, and the

visitors like us have to eat, so it's only right."

Sugah marveled at the workers and complimented them, "Thank yall for a good meal. Thank

Yall for feeding the folks who work here and the Daddies waiting on their babies to be born."

After 3 weeks, Jana and her baby girl were ready to go home. Jana refused to name

the baby, so Arlene had them put Camille on the birth certificate. Camille was Arlene's

grandmother's name. It fit her perfectly. Camille had rosy cheeks and a marvelous coo.

She rarely cried unless her diaper needed to be changed or if she had gas on her tummy.

She also had a strong grip when she held Arlene's fingers. Arlene had bonded with Camille. The

hospital had allowed her to use a separate room to spend time with Camille, once they

understood Jana had been raped. Each day a different nurse would take Sugah to the

hospital cafeteria for lunch. The employees fell in love with Sugah and the manager gave her

a tour of the kitchen. Sugah surprised them all by saying, "One day I think I will work here.

I helped my mama was dishes since I was old enough to walk. I will be good at it." Everyone

smiled as the manager gave her an application. "When you are 17 and you still want to work

here. We will give you a job."

Sugah was so happy, that she hugged every one of the employees and the manager. She ran

back to Arlene to tell her the great news. "Mama! I got a job!"

Arlene said, "Sugah what do you mean?"

"It's washing dishes in the restaurant, I mean the cafeteria as they call it. The manager gave me

An application and as soon as I turn 17 I can work here if I want to."

Arlene hugged Sugah and told her, "Honey that is wonderful news. It is something wonderful to

Look forward to."

When Jana was awake Arlene spent time with her and Sugah. The hospital had a television in the

Room. It was fascinating to watch shows like Mash, Sandford and Son, and The Price Is Right

Sugah said, "Mama we need one of these televisions. We can watch TV. at home."

Arlene laughed and said, "Sugah we are busy women, we don't have no time for

Watching TV, We got things to do. How you gone collect all your eggs, when you sitting down

With your face in the TV? How you gone make your rounds checking on all your friends, if your

face is in the TV?"

Sugah thought for a minute and said, "Okay mama. I understand. But maybe one day we could

get one, I would really like it."

Arlene had fixed a place in the corner of her room for the baby bed. She had put up a mobile for

Camille to play with and attached a window pane to the wall with pictures of the family

attached to the glass.

The pastor stopped by with flowers for Jana. Jana thanked him but was weary. She was tired, she

still hurting and she was sad. The pastor met the baby and then gave Arlene some encouraging

words. "I know it's unorthodox Arlene but the ladies' auxiliary has had a baby shower without

you. They will bring the presents and food to your house. They didn't want to upset Jana

by having the baby shower and asking y'all to be there, so they are bringing it to you. Only 2

women and 4 men are coming over to drop everything off. Hopefully, Jana will be asleep when

they come. They are scheduled to come tonight at 8:45. Arlene your church loves you and

wants you to know how much you mean to us."

Arlene cried and hugged the Pastor. "Sir I can't thank you enough."

Sugah tried to keep her company but Jana kept falling asleep. Arlene had put a small

radio in her room so she would not hear Camille cry.

After dinner, Arlene sent the girls to bathe and get ready for bed. Neither argued with her.

Promptly at 8:45, Arlene opened the door and a parade of ladies and men entered her house.

The presents were clothes for the baby. It seemed like a hundred outfits, bottles, Diapers, Burp

Cloths, Baby Lotion, Baby Oil, Diaper pail, Diaper bag, Baby bathtub, toys, and more clothing.

There were 3 presents for Jana and for Sugah. Arlene agreed to let them open them the next

Day, as they were asleep.

There was so much food, that Arlene worried she wouldn't be able to contain it all in her

refrigerator.

Arlene burst into tears and thanked her church family. "I know that you love me and I want

Ya to know, I adore and love you. Please continue to pray for my family, including my boys.

God will bless each of you for helping us I love you all."

The next morning the girls were surprised at their gifts. Arlene had moved all of the other items

for the baby into her room. She cleared out a dresser drawer to put the baby's clothes in. She

thanked God for his protection and for providing all of her needs.

Surprise!!

The next day, Cullen Markly, one of Arlene's neighbors came by to talk to Arlene in private.

Arlene got Jana settled into bed after lunch and put the baby in her bassinet rolling it out to

he porch where she and Cullen sat.

She poured some tea for her and Cullen. He was leaning over the bassinet. "My goodness

Arlene, she looks like an angel. She's so beautiful. God is so good."

Cullen sat back up and said, "Arlene, that man in that truck came around again while y'all were

gone. He kept circling, spinning his wheels. He almost run me over. I just brought out my

shotgun and blew out his back glass. I might have taken out his tail lights too. You know I am a

pretty good shot. The way he hollered, he got some of the shotgun pellets. I think I sent a

pretty good message to him."

Arlene laughed heartily. "Cullen you are such a great friend. I pray that is the last

we hear from him. "

Cullen cleared his throat and asked, "Do y'all need anything, Arlene?"

Arlene said, "Hmmm. Well, you could stay here with the girls or go to the grocery

store for me."

Cullen blushed and said, "I'll wait while you make me out your grocery list."

Arlene laughed and said, "Its just a few things like milk, butter, buttermilk, and bacon.

"You have to stay for dinner. The church brought over so much food last night, my refrigerator is

Bursting. Please say you will stay for dinner?"

"Id be delighted Arlene."

Arlene warmed up 3 casseroles, made a pitcher of tea, and it was all ready when Cullen came

back from the Piggly Wiggly. She ran to look out the window when she heard someone pull up.

Arlene put a hand over her chest, relieved that it was Cullen and not the dirty guy coming for

Jana and the baby.

They all ate a good meal. Arlene put a plate back for Jana since she was sleeping, and fixed a

lunch plate for Cullen to take to work the next day. Sugah agreed to do the dishes.

The baby started to cry, so Arlene changed her and fed her.. Cullen offered to help Sugah with

the dishes. Afterward, Arlene made coffee for her and Cullen while Sugah took a bath.

Cullen said, "Thank you for dinner it was delicious. It sure beats crackers and Vienna sausages."

Arlene gasped and said, "Cullen, don't be eating that for dinner. Come over here and eat with

us. I always got plenty. Why, Vienna sausage and crackers is just a snack, that's not enough to

fill a grown man up."

Cullen chuckled, "I didn't mean to rile you up."

Arlene blushed, "Well folks have to eat."

Cullen put down his coffee and said, "Arlene. I have a proposition for you. I hope you will hear

me out. You, girls, are over here like a sitting duck for that heathen to come back and hurt y'all.

I can't live with myself if something happens to any of you. I, I love you, Arlene. I loved you

since before Rascal died. You remember how I used to make you paper flowers in school?"

Arlene smiled and said, "I remember Cullen. I saved all of those for years in a hope chest

my mama gave me. Rascal just happened to ask me to marry first, since you dragged your feet."

Cullen sighed and said, "I'm still kicking myself over that. I was trying to get my courage up. I

really didn't have anything to offer you but I loved you, still do."

Arlene put her hand on his arm, "Cullen, I'm older now."

A big smile came across his face, "We are both older Arlene, but we can help Jana raise that

baby and continue to raise Sugah. We got a lot of good years left in us."

"I don't know if Jana is gonna want the baby. She's so damaged from what happened to her."

She proceeded to share Jana's story. Cullen had tears rolling down his face, he pulled out his

handkerchief to wipe Arlene's face and then his. "I hate that happened to Jana. I wish now I had

killed that monster. But we could free her from the hardship of being a parent. She could be a

big sister to Camille. We could put Jana in school when she is ready. There is a technical school

2 towns over from here. We could set her up in her own apartment, of course only if she wants it.

Arlene, I ran into the pastor of your church and told him I was going to propose to you tonight.

He gave us his blessing if I start coming to church with you. And I gotta get saved. He said you

deserve a good Christian man. I told him I was willing to do anything to have you as my wife.

He then corrected me and said you need to give your heart to Jesus not just for the perks. So right

'There in his office, I did it, I accepted Christ as my Savior, and I'm getting baptized Sunday after

church. I hope you will be there as a witness to my being born again."

Arlene was speechless but she nodded yes vigorously.

"He has agreed to marry us once I wear you down. Will you say yes?"

Arlene searched his face, "Are you sure Cullen? I come with a lot of responsibilities."

"Positively, absolutely, without a doubt, any of your burdens, I will gladly share." He said with a

smile.

He got down on one knee and pulled a ring from his pants pocket.

"It was my mother's ring, Arlene. Will you marry me?"

Arlene got down on the floor with him, and held his hands in hers, "Yes Cullen. I will marry you."

He put the stunning diamond and ruby ring on her finger and they kissed.

Sugah walked in on them kissing and said, "Ewww what's going on here? Y'all sexually active?"

Arlene yelled, "Sugah! Don't be asking folks that."

Arlene and Cullen helped each other up off the floor. Both were giggling about Sugah's question.

Cullen said, "Sugah remember when I asked your permission to marry your mama, and you said,

it was okay with you?"

Sugah nodded her head and said, "Yes sir, but I didn't know you gone kiss her."

Cullen and Arlene laughed and hugged Sugah. "That is what married folks do Sugah."

Sugah shrugged her shoulders and said, "Well okay then. "

The baby started cooing and they played with her. Cullen held her for the first time.

Suddenly they were surprised by a knock at the door. Arlene held her breath, andshe peaked out

the window, but it wasn't the dirty guy it was Sheriff Ezell. Cullen stepped outside to speak to

him. He explained everything that Jana had told her mother.

"Well, we got the report from the counselor over in Webo, so when Jana is able if you could

bring her to the sheriff's office so we can take her statement, then yall can give us a description

of the guy and his vehicle."

"There seems to be a lot of these guys involved Sheriff. They put the kidnapped girls on the

street as prostitutes and take their money. Jana told her mama if those girls don't make a

certain amount of money, the men holding them, won't let them eat. They didn't put Jana

on the street, the main guy pretended to marry her and keep her for himself.

He came by here 5 months ago, looking for Jana, and Arlene and her Bible scared him off. He

came back again, and me and Betty blew out his back glass and maybe his tail lights. "

The sheriff grinned because he knew Betty was a shotgun. "Lord, what is this world coming to?"

Cullen said, "It's getting worse every day. I'm gonna do my best to keep all of these girls safe."

The sheriff shook Cullen's hand and said, "I know you will do a good job."

"I asked Arlene to marry me. She said yes!

"The sheriff shook his hand and said, "All right Cullen, congratulations to you both!"

Arlene came out and asked the sheriff if he wanted a glass of tea.

"No gal, I better get going. I will see you all soon. Congratulations on your engagement."

They smiled and thanked him, as he walked to his patrol car.

Arlene looked at Cullen and said, "Jana dislikes the baby. She said today that she can't stand to

look at her because she looks like the dirty man." I asked her if she wanted to hold her and she

said, "No ma'am. I'd rather not." Then she turned her back to the baby while I picked her up. I

told her, "Jana, that baby is not to blame for who her father is. You shouldn't take it out on her."

Jana ran to her room sobbing. I went behind her and told her that we are going to raise the

Baby. It will be like a sister or a cousin to her. I told her you asked me to marry you and I

accepted. She grabbed me and hugged me. I think she is really happy for us."

"Mama please don't be mad at me. Something is wrong with me. I only feel love for you and

Sugah. l feel like a statue. Even at church, I don't feel like Jesus hears my prayers. I'm too

filthy inside my mind. No decent man will ever want me. I will be an old maid, living here,

in your way. Oh, Mama. Why can't I forget? Arlene asked her, "Baby is possible you haven't

told her everything that happened,"

"I have told everything I remember but I have dreams that they are coming to kill us, and I can't stop it."

# 2 months pass

Arlene and Cullen spend the next 2 months attending weekly marriage counseling with the

Pastor of her church. Finally, he felt like they were prepared for a good marriage. The following

Sunday after church they were married at 4 pm. The entire church attended. The Ladies

Auxiliary decorated the church conference room, they provided a beautiful reception and even

provided a Wedding cake. Margie Tillman made Arlene 2 wedding bouquets. One to throw and

one to keep.

Arlene threw it high in the air and Jana caught it. Sugah got mad because she wanted to

catch it. Jana handed it to her. Sugah smelled the fake flowers and gave them back to Jana. The

lady's auxiliary had prepared a feast for the reception. A 3 piece quartet provided music for the event. It was very elegant. Cullen gave a very large donation to the Pastor and the head of the lady's auxiliary. Jana and Sugah spent the night with Darlene Sampson. The baby stayed overnight with Sister Mackey and her husband and, Arlene, and Cullen, stayed in a hotel for their honeymoon overnight.

# 3 months later

Jana was finally mentally able to give her statement to the sheriff. She and Cullen met with

The special operations unit handled kidnapping and other personal assault crimes.

The Sergeant, Robert Lancaster, excused himself stating he wasn't feeling well. A different

Sergeant came in to take Jana's statement. Jana gave them all the names she could

remember and warrants were drawn up for their arrest.

Afterward, she and Cullen met with a Crime artist who drew a composite of the dirty man.

When he showed Jana the picture, she gasped and then fainted.

Cullen spoke up and said, "Okay, she has had enough. I am taking her home. I think she has

told you all she remembers." He and another deputy helped Jana to his truck. Arlene put her

to bed. Jana slept until Arlene woke her up to eat that afternoon. The family all went to

Wednesday night Bible study. There was a new guy there. Jana thought she recognized him and

it gave her anxiety because she couldn't place him; she asked Arlene to take her home.

The next afternoon, there was a knock at the door. Cullen was at work. Arlene peeked outside

and saw a deputy sheriff. She answered the door. "Hello, officer. I don't believe Jana is able to

talk about what happened to her. She's feeling poorly."

He smiled and said, "I'm here on a personal matter. I was going to speak to you all at church last night but you left before I could. I'm Robert Lancaster. I would like to ask Jana on a date."

Arlene looked surprised and said, "Let me go ask Jana if she is up to talking to you. Have a

seat on the porch rocker. I will be right back."

He smiled and said, "Yes ma'am."

In a few minutes, Arlene opened the door and told him to come in. "Jana will be out in a few

minutes Robert." She handed him a glass of sweet tea.

Sugah came in and kept him company until Jana got there.

"Hey Sugah. How are you doing? I'm Amanda's brother Robert. Do you Remember me? How have you been?"

"I'm okay. Yes, I think I remember you." She said as she looked him over. "You ever shoot anybody with that gun Robert?"

"Robert smiled and said, "No Sugah, and I pray I never have to."

Sugah asked him, "Why did you want to be a sheriff when you growed up?"

Robert looked at her serious and said, "I just like helping people, and I don't like bad guys."

Sugah nodded her head, suggesting she understood, however, she thought it was stupid

to have a gun if you didn't plan on shooting people.

After a few more minutes, Jana came into the room.

She was wearing blue jeans and a pretty top, and her hair was in a ponytail.

Robert stood up, "My goodness Jana you look beautiful today. Do

you remember me? I'm Amanda's brother. Y'all used to play softball together."

Jana said, "Yes, Robert! I remember you. How are you doing?"

Sugah left the room. Bored with the conversation.

Robert beamed and said, "I'm good. I came to your church last night hoping to talk to you.

Cullen invited me. I was wondering if you might like to go to dinner with me one night."

Jana dropped her head and said, "Why me? You don't want me, Robert. I'm damaged goods."

"No, you are not. Something terrible happened to you. Yes, you were a victim but you survived.

You are not a victim anymore Jana, you are a survivor. All of that was in the past. It's over and

done. You are a beautiful young lady with a lot of good living to do. I want to be a part of your

life."

Jana put her hands over her face. Robert reached and pulled her hands down into his.

"Jana, I have loved you for years. I could just never tell you. Amanda was afraid it would mess

up your friendship. So, I held back. Now we are all adults and I can tell you how I feel. I still feel that love for you. I know you love animals, especially horses. I have 3 horses and 2 donkeys on my farm. My father passed away and left me the farm. It's really beautiful. I have a large

vegetable garden and a beautiful herb garden. Oh, and I have 16 chickens. Amanda planted

a lot of beautiful roses and we have house plants, oh a few small goats, and one milking cow.

Amanda is getting married soon and she would like to see you.

She misses your friendship. I remodeled the house; it is so pretty now. I think I did a good job."

Jana was smiling but didn't know what to say?"

Arlene entered the living room and asked Robert to stay for dinner. He looked at Jana and she

smiled and said, "Yes, please do."

"I'm on my lunch break now, I get off at 5:30, so I will hurry back here then."

Arlene said, "That sounds good. We will see you then."

Robert smiled at Jana and said, "See you soon." And walked out the door.

Jana was in shock. She sat on the sofa looking at her mother. "What just happened Mama?"

Arlene smiled and said, "A decent young man just paid you a visit. Jana good people don't

hold grudges or hold your past against you. There are still good people in this world. Now go

take a bath and get prettied up. Robert is very handsome. "

As soon as Cullen got home and showered, Robert arrived and they all had dinner. Robert had

taken off his gun belt and placed it between his feet because Sugah was giving him dirty looks.

She did not like guns or maybe she just didn't understand the concept of carrying one.

Sugah moved the tablecloth to find out exactly where the gun was and Robert winked at her.

Sugah rolled her eyes, and then Robert chuckled.

Jana was quiet during dinner, but she had a happy look on her face and was listening intently to

all of the conversations. Every time Robert asked her a question, she responded and smiled.

Arlene asked Jana to serve the chocolate cake for dessert. Jana looked surprised but jumped up

to handle the task.

Sugah went into the kitchen. "I will fix the coffee for you, Jana. Mama taught me how to do it. 6

of the smaller spoons of coffee, and fill it up to here with water." She pointed to the fill line but

Jana wasn't looking. "Don't forget to plug it in. And you have to put the creamer and sugar on the table. Are you listening to me?" Sugah asked accusingly.

"No Sugah. I'm sorry. I was thinking about something else."

"Fine, I will handle it!" Sugah said.

Jana apologized and Sugah just sighed and finished gathering the things for the coffee.

"Why did you get only 4 cups and saucers?" Jana asked.

"Because there are 4 adults Jana. I am only 13 years old. Do you think I want to drink that

crap?"

Jana laughed and said, "No I guess not. You are so grown actin', I forget you are still a young'un."

Sugah put saucers for the cake, the coffee cups, creamer, and sugar on a tray and carried it

to the dining room table.

Jana brought the cake, then the coffee.

Robert smiled at her in a way that made her feel very special. Like a real grown-up. He retold

the story about his farm and invited them all to come ride his horses.

Sugah perked up and raised her hand. "I am interested. When is this gonna happen?"

Arlene said, "After we get to know Robert better, now pipe down." Everyone laughed.

After dessert, the men went outside to talk.

Cullen spoke up, "I remember you left the interrogation area when we arrived. I believe you

said you didn't feel well and excused yourself."

"That is correct sir. When I saw Jana, all those feelings I had for her came flooding back.

I went straight to the Sheriff to speak to him about recusing me from the investigation.

I told him I wanted his permission to marry Jana. He told me I had to ask you and Ms. Arlene, and he was fine with it. He also explained it may take some time to win her heart because

of all she has been through. He encouraged me to start as friends, which is what I intend to do."

Cullen said, "The sheriff is a good man. He stopped by my job to tell me that you had spoken to

him. He put in a very good word for your character Robert. You have done a good job for his

department. He even said you were to be promoted soon to Lieutenant."

Robert's eyes opened wide, and he said, "I just took the test a week ago. I guess that means I

passed it." He smiled a big smile. Then Tristan put out his hand to shake it.

As Cullen shook his hand, Robert said, "I want to earn her heart, sir. I have loved her for so long."

"I think you will make a fine husband for our Jana. However, you are going to need a lot of

patience and love."

"Yes sir, I understand. I didn't even know Jana was back in town until you two arrived to

give a statement. I will do whatever it takes to win her over. She's beautiful and kind. I

remember seeing her so happy many times with my sister."

Cullen smiled and said, "You two will make your own memories. I think you should come to

dinner 3 times a week for a couple of months to let her get reacquainted with you."

Cullen said, "Yes sir that is a great idea. Thank you."

They went back inside and had a pleasant talk with the ladies. Cullen told a story about him

and Robert's father, Wilbur.

"We went duck hunting in Lankly County one Saturday morning. It was freezing cold. Neither of

us had packed a duck caller, the thing you blow in to attract the ducks. So, Wilbur started

whistling and blowing into his hands. I started laughing so hard. He sounded ridiculous. If any

ducks were listening, they were probably laughing too. Then Wilbur got to laughing. We didn't

know a bunch of ducks were bedded down right by us, and when we started laughing, they all

flew right over our heads. We couldn't get to our guns in time and we didn't get one duck to

take home. It was hilarious, we laughed all the way home."

The story made everyone laugh. Robert wiped a tear away and said, "I sure miss my father. He

was a great man."

Cullen said, "Yes he was Robert."

Robert explained to Cullen the changes he had made to the farm and the additional animals.

Cullen said," Our Jana loves animals."

Jana spoke up and said, "Especially horses. They seem so calming and smart."

Cullen smiled and said, "They are gentle giants. I really like horses. The donkeys are

more ornery and stubborn. They both like to be brushed but they act like they don't. Funny thing if you are brushing them and stop, they get offended."

Everyone laughed.

Cullen said, "Sounds like some..." Arlene threw him a look and he didn't finish his thought.

Everyone laughed again.

Robert told Arlene and Cullen thank you for the dinner and told Sugah and Jana that the dessert

was delicious. He smiled all the way home.

Every payday, Robert gave Cullen an envelope with 75 dollars. Cullen protested but Robert

said, "I know it costs extra to feed another grown man."

Cullen told him, "I will put this towards the wedding cost then."

Robert smiled and said, " I hope it's everything Jana ever wanted. She is warming up to me. I'm

so thankful. My heart just about bursts out of my chest every time I see her."

"She has begun talking about you when you are not there, and she is always smiling. She looks forward to seeing you, Robert."

For three months, Robert was there for dinner, Monday, Wednesday and Friday.

He always changed into regular clothes so he didn't upset Sugah with his gun.

He sat with the family, next to Jana every Sunday morning and Wednesday evening at the

church. No one knew it but he always had a backup weapon on his back in case anyone tried to hurt Jana while he was present.

After 3 months, Jana was actively engaging in the conversations and sitting alone with Robert on

the porch after dinner.

He asked Cullen if he could invite all of them over the coming Saturday for a barbecue and

to see the farm.

"I was promoted today to Lieutenant. I guess that calls for a family celebration. And Amanda has been asking to see Jana."

Cullen agreed and congratulated Robert with a hug. "I'm proud of you Son."

"That's wonderful Robert! What can we bring?" Arlene asked.

"Well ordinarily I would say nothing, but your banana pudding is out of this world."

Arlene laughed and said, "Well, Jana has been making for the last 3 months. But I'm sure she's

gonna be happy to whip you some up."

Jana blushed and said, "Yes of course I will bring it. I can't wait to see Amanda too. I have

missed her so much."

Sugah looked worried and spoke up, "You mean we gonna see horses and donkeys? I mean I

never rode no horse or donkey...what will I do? How will I do it?"

Robert smiled and said, "I will be there to help you Sugah. I think we are just gonna ride the

horses and look at the donkeys."

Sugah shook her head to say that was okay with her.

Jana spoke up and said, "Sugah, your whole family is gonna be there. Robert will take care of

us."

Sugah shrugged her shoulders and said, "He better, Daddy Cullen will take care of him if he don't."

Everyone laughed. Cullen spoke up, "Sugah I've ridden horses before. It's a lot of fun."

Sugah looked skeptical but finally agreed. "I will try it but if I don't like it, I won't try anymore."

Robert hugged her and said, "I would never let anything bad happen to any of you."

Sugah said, "Don't hug me, Robert. Did I ask for a hug? You just make sure the horses like me."

"I promise it will be fine. The horses are very gentle."

Sugah said, "I'm going to take my bath mama then I'm headed to bed."

Everyone said goodnight.

Robert left Jana sitting in the living room with Cullen and Arlene.

"I think Robert likes me. I like him too. I am happy I am going to see Amanda. She was my best

friend for so many years. We grew up together at school. When were kids she didn't want me and

Robert to be boyfriend and girlfriend. I always told her he was handsome and she was kinda

jealous. I think she was scared we wouldn't be best friends anymore.

We was just kids. I am excited to see the farm too. Robert says he has put a lot of work into it."

Cullen said, "I'm off to bed. You girls don't stay up too long. I love y'all." He hugged Jana and

started to walk away.

"Hey, where's my hug?" Arlene called out.

"You come and get yours sweetheart." Cullen teased.

The women giggled. "Mama, you seem so happy now. It's hard-pressed to remember before you

had Cullen as a husband. He is a good man. I am so happy for you. Do you think Robert could

love me one day?"

"He already does Jana. He has been taking it slow on the advice of Cullen, so as to not

scare you away."

"I'm not scared of him. I feel like my life is right when I'm with him. I'm excited about Saturday.

what do I wear?"

"Well, you can wear jeans since you are gonna be riding a horse. You look good in anything."

"I hope Amanda can forgive me for disappearing."

"Baby don't even think about that. God has turned your whole life around."

"He really has Mama. I don't feel the pain and the guilt that I had when I came home. I know I

haven't said it but thank you and Cullen for raising ...Ellen. It was the first time in almost a

year she had said the baby's name. I'm sorry that I couldn't be her mother.

There is just too much pain associated with her. That is what my counselor said. You are such an

amazing mother to take on that responsibility. I hope I turn out just like you Mama."

Arlene reached for Jana's hands and held them. "Baby you have been through so much. No one

could blame you for what you have suffered. Just keep trusting in God Jana. He has never failed

us. He brought you home. Cullen and I happily agreed to raise Ellen as our own. I pray you

can accept her as your sister."

***

When Saturday came, everyone was excited to go to Robert's for the picnic. Cullen had bought

cowboy hats and cowboy boots for Ellen, Sugah, and Jana.

Sugah was asking a million questions about horses. "Do they bite? Do they lay down to sleep?

Do they talk to each other? How do they brush their teeth? How will I know if they don't like

me?"

Arlene tried to be calm and reassuring to Sugah. "Honey, we have to wait and see if Robert can

answer any of your questions."

Cullen just smiled and shook his head.

As they pulled up to the Lancaster Farm, Cullen was very impressed.

It had a double gate that had 2 metal horseheads welded onto the gate. It was stunning. Above

the top was a sign that said, Lancaster Farm.

the entire front was fenced in. Robert was waiting to let them in. He opened the door and asked

Sugah to step out of the car and ride to the house in his golf cart with him. Sugah asked Arlene if

it was okay. "But of course, honey, go ahead. It will be great fun!"

They got in the golf cart. Robert showed her the handle to hold onto and he showed her how to

use the pedal to make the cart move, and the one to make it stop. He also showed her the reverse.

"I never been in one of these before. I hope it donn go too fast." Sugah said with a frown on her

face.

Robert said, "No it doesn't go fast Sugah but it keeps me from walking from the gate to the

house. It's a little way to the house."

"So, it's too far to walk?" Sugah asked.

Robert chuckled and said, "Yes, that's what I was trying to tell you."

"I figured it out," Sugah said, she had a smug look on her face.

He drove slowly and Cullen followed him in the car. Sugah was impressed but she had a firm

grip on the handle. She watched him intensely.

The farm was a showplace. It was absolutely stunning. There were 2 barns and multiple sheds

for tools and feed. The grounds were taken very good care of and the animals were serene.

The grassy fields were lush and green. Several sections were fenced in for the various animals.

They pulled up to the barn and parked there. Everyone got out to take the tour.

Robert walked everyone around to show them the gardens. He had 2 corrals that he let the

Horses and donkeys play in. The goats roamed free on the property, and although their area was

fenced, he couldn't keep them in if he tried.

Arlene loved the gardens and Cullen congratulated Robert on what a great accomplishment

he had performed.

"Son, I remember when this was nothing but dirt roads and trees. Me and your Daddy would

fish over there (pointing towards a pond) for 8 hours at a time. Your Mama would say, 'Don't

y'all come back here with no fish, or y'all are eating hushpuppies and fried taters for dinner.' We

always came back with a big mess of fish."

Robert laughed, "Yes, I remember y'all fishing. Y'all are legends. Daddy had to keep that pond

stocked up."

Cullen laughed and said, "Yes we were a lot better fishermen than hunters."

All of a sudden, Sugah came around the corner on the golf cart. She was driving the thing.

"Wee, look a here yall. I can drive."

Robert called her over and she stopped right in front of him.

"Sugah how did you figure out how to drive this thing?"

"Well duh Robert, you showed me when I got in. You think I'm daff? I can do things."

Robert held his hands up and said, "I know you can Sugah, just drive a little slower when taking

those corners, and don't be chasing the goats."

Sugah looked sad and said, "Oh man, that was what I was gone do next."

Everyone laughed, yet Arlene had a tiny panic attack.

Arlene carried Ellen to see the chickens and goats. Robert joined her. "I hope Jana
will learn to love it here."

"She will Robert. Look at her face. She is amazed. I haven't seen her so happy in a long time.
She returns your love."

They all went into the house. It was stunning. Robert had done an amazing job remodeling the
house too. After he showed them everything. They all went to the back deck to start the
barbecue. Cullen got the banana pudding out of the car and put it in the refrigerator.

Robert had hamburgers, hot dogs, and chicken to cook on the grill. He had already made
the potato salad, baked beans, and corn on the cob.

Jana asked if she could help Robert on the grill and he said, "Why yes ma'am you can. You can
baste the chicken with this sauce and turn it every 4 minutes or so, so it doesn't burn."

Jana smiled and was happy to help.

Cullen, Arlene, and the baby sat at the patio table and Robert got them all sweet tea.

Arlene asked if she could help with anything and Robert told her, "No ma'am you just relax
and enjoy this beautiful day. Ellen was very content and was enjoying herself too. She
wanted Cullen to hold her. She was a happy baby.

Robert teased Jana, "I just want you to know if you burn that chicken, I'm still gonna eat it since
you cooked it."

Jana laughed and said, "I'm a good cook Robert. I won't burn the chicken. You will see. The

the trick is not to leave it."

Robert winked at her and she blushed.

Cullen had brought his guitar and played several songs. He was serenading Arlene and she was

beaming. Cullen had a beautiful voice and everyone clapped when he finished each song. Sugah

whizzed by on the golf cart. Robert called to her, "Sugah we are going to eat in about 20

minutes. Don't forget to come back to eat."

Sugah was having the time of her life. She waved to all of them and yelled, "Yeehaw!"

Cullen said, "Well Robert, now you've done it. I'm gonna have to buy a farm and a golf cart."

Robert laughed and said, "This farm brings me great joy. I didn't show you but I have a shooting

range set up down by the creek. Sugah hates my gun, so I was hesitant to bring it up."

Arlene spoke up and said, "I don't know where she gets that response from. We have never had

guns and she has never been exposed to them. But she don't like them. She asked me a

hundred questions about you carrying a gun. I just told her you were a law officer and you have

to carry a gun in case you need to protect someone or stop a bad man. I can't explain her

objection."

Cullen said, "Some people just don't like different things that they don't understand. It is okay.

She will get used to you in uniform. I have guns but she has never seen them"

Jana called out, "Robert, the chicken is ready." She plated it up and put foil over it to keep it

warm.

Robert said, "Jana, you did a great job. I might eat all that chicken by myself."

Cullen said, "Now wait a minute Son you got company. You got to share!"

Everyone laughed.

Robert put the hot dogs and hamburgers on the grill. Jana went inside and cut up the

lettuce, tomatoes, and onions, then brought them outside. Robert smiled at her and said,

"You know we make a great team." Jana smiled a big smile. He kissed her cheek.

Cullen went to go find Sugah. She was stopped in front of a corral that had horses inside of it.

She was mesmerized, so deep in thought she didn't hear Cullen calling her name. She jumped

when he got into the cart with her.

"Daddy Cullen, you almost give me a heart attack."

Cullen said, "Oh baby girl. I didn't mean to startle you. It's time to eat. What do you think of

those horses?"

Sugah turned to him and said, "They are the prettiest things I ever seen in my life."

Tears were rolling down her cheeks.

Cullen got his handkerchief out and wiped her tears. He understood her feelings. He felt that

way the first time and the last time he saw her mother only a few minutes ago.

They sat there for a few minutes, then Cullen said, "We need to go eat lunch. Robert and

Jana has fixed a feast for us."

Sugah started up the cart and took them to the patio.

Cullen said to Arlene, "Baby doll, I have some good news and bad news."

Arlene smiled and asked, "What is it, honey?"

"Well, the good news is Sugah fell in love with the horses, the bad news is, we gonna have

to buy her some."

Arlene laughed and said, "Cullen, where are we gonna keep a horse?"

Cullen said, "I guess I will just have to buy the Adam's farm about 4 miles from here."

Arlene looked stunned, "Have you already bought that farm, Cullen?"

He said, "Yes baby I have. It will be our new home. It had a nice house that I know will be a

great place to raise Sugah and Ellen. It has a barn that can hold 4 horses, a chicken house

for your chickens, a rooster house in case you want baby chickens, and a creek that runs through

the back like Roberts. There is even a pond for fishing."

Arlene burst into tears; they were happy tears. "I love you, Cullen."

"I love you Arlene and all of our family. Shoot I even love Robert."

"I love you buddy. Thank you for making me a part of your family." Robert said with a smile.

Jana hugged Robert and said, "You are a part of this family. I love you."

Robert dropped to his knee and fished out a diamond ring. "Jana, will you do me the

honor of being my wife?"

Jana put her hands up to her face, then lowered them and showed him her smile.

"Yes, Robert. I will be your wife." Jana said as tears flowed down her face.

Everyone yelled, "Congratulations!" Except Sugah, she yelled, 'Yall gone have sexual

relations?"

Arlene yelled, "Sugah, stop that!"

Sugah stood her ground and said, "You are the ones who said married people do it."

Arlene said, "Sugah it is not nice to talk about that subject in public." Everyone was holding

their sides to keep from laughing.

They finally got to their lunch. It was delicious. Everyone ate a lot and complimented Jana and

Robert on their combined cooking skills.

Sugah became sleepy after she had eaten so much. Arlene took her and Ellen into the guest

house to take a nap. The girls fell asleep almost instantly. Cullen joined Arlene. He brought her a

cup of coffee and they sat on the little patio that was attached to the cottage.

"Arlene, are you excited about our farm?"

"Yes, my love. I can hardly wait to make it our own."

"Robert found out about it and told me about it. The owners were eager to sell so they could

move to Florida to be near their kids. I got a great deal on it. I even bought the livestock.

Sugah is going to be over the moon happy when she sees it. Robert brought some of his

friends to help repair the roof of the barn. One of them rewired the electric box in the other barn.

I tried to pay all of them and none of them would take my money. I have a sneaky suspicion

Robert paid them. That boy, sure is a blessing to our family. I am so happy Jana said yes to

his proposal. I don't think he was planning on doing it today, but when opportunity strikes you

have to go for it. I think it will make Jana feel better us being so close to them too."

Arlene said, "Mister, you are just full of surprises. How did I get so lucky?"

Cullen stood up and kissed her. "I'm the lucky one Darling."

After the girls woke up, Arlene stayed behind to clean up from the lunch. Robert protested but

she insisted. Everyone else went to the corral where the horses were. Of course, Sugah rode the

golf cart over there.

Robert brought the 2 most gentle horses from the barn. He and Cullen saddled them up.

Sugah was trembling with excitement and fear. The horse she was to ride was named Breezy.

To Sugah, Breezy was 12 ft tall, but she wasn't really.

Robert told Sugah to spend some time talking to Breezy.

"Now Robert just what in the world would I talk to a horse about?"

Robert smiled and said, "Tell her about you and your family. Tell her things you like to do. She

will understand you. Horses are smart"

Sugah shrugged her shoulders then she just about talked that poor horse's ears off.

She brushed her and braided her mane.

"I'd like to ride you Miss Breezy but I'm still kinda scared," Sugah admitted to the horse.

Breezy knelt down almost to the ground, so Sugah could get on her saddle. Robert was

watching and told Sugah, "Go ahead, honey. She's inviting you to ride."

Sugah said, "I aint your honey. You gone marry my sister. Just call me Sugah."

Robert quickly said, "I apologize Sugah. You are right to correct me."

Sugah threw her right leg over the saddle and got a good grip on the horn of the saddle.

Breezy raised slowly and had the reins in her mouth. She turned towards Sugah and

Sugah took the reins from her. Breezy went in a slow, easy walk around the corral.

For a minute Robert was speechless. It was like nothing he had ever seen. Breezy was

teaching Sugah how to ride her. Robert rushed over, he had been busy putting Jana's saddle

on and admiring her beauty. Robert called out calmly, "Sugah if you want her to turn, you pull

on the rein, left or right. If you want her to stop, you say Halt or Stop and tighten your legs and

pull the reins toward you. Do you understand?"

Sugah smiled and said, "Yes sir. I think me and her have it figured out."

Jana went to get her mama. She had to see this. Sugah was riding like she had done it all

her life.

Arlene cried when she saw her baby on that horse. For one thing, the horse looked majestic, and

for another, Sugah was like a professional rider. They galloped, Breezy did some fancy dancing, they moved in circles, Sugah whispered in her ear and Breezy bowed. Everyone clapped. It was

amazing to watch. After about 30 minutes, Breezy knelt all the way down and Sugah

dismounted. She kissed Breezy as she started to stand.

Cullen and Robert were astounded.

Somehow Robert found his voice and said, "Sugah lead her to the barn and I will show you how

to take off her saddle."

To his amazement, Sugah understood the steps and took off the saddle then put it back on several

times to show she knew how to do it.

Sugah had a huge smile on her face. "I put Breezy in her stall, Daddy Cullen. I gave her some

hay and some water. I think we gone get on just fine."

Cullen hugged Sugah and said, "You did great baby girl."

Jana rode NOLA, a gentle horse Robert had rescued from New Orleans. Jana was nervous but

still had a pleasant ride. It was only about 10 minutes long but still, it was fun. Cullen walked

alongside of her. Jana said, "I am not a natural like Sugah."

"You will learn and become more comfortable sweetheart. I can tell you love horses."

"I truly do Robert. I think they are magical."

Robert smiled at her and said, "Your smile is magical Jana. I love you so much."

"I love you too sweetheart."

"I suppose I was just a little too nervous."

"Its okay baby. Next time just talke to her and show her your engagement ring. It will enlighten the mood. You will get to know her as you spend time with her every day, I promise. She will learn to love you as I do baby."

Jana smiled and hugged Robert.


Arlene was eager to see their new farm, however, the men who were revarnishing the wood

Floors were not finished. So, they said it would take another 5 days for all the work to be

completed.

Cullen and Robert met over there at morning and dinner time to feed the animals.

"Son, I can't tell you how much I appreciate all you have done to help me."

"Think nothing of it, sir, we are family, "Robert assured him.

"How is going with Jana?"

"Sir, she has taken to me like a moth to a flame. I honestly believe she loves me now. The

engagement seemed to turn on a light in her heart. I am so happy and so is she."

"I'm happy for y'all. But Robert remember to keep God in y'all's marriage. Arlene and I have

Bible study together and we even pray together at night. If I go to bed early, I can't fall

asleep until she comes in to pray with me."

"Oh wow, that is powerful advice, Cullen. I will discuss this with Jana. It is important, especially

after all she has been through."

Cullen smiled and said, "Lord, Arlene is so excited and happy for y'all. She has already taken

Jana shopping for new dishes, glasses, utensils, and things for the kitchen. She wants to make it

her own."

Robert laughed and said, "Bless her heart, she asked me if she could redecorate and I told her

'Baby you change anything you want to. This is your house too."

Cullen shook his head, "Women and shopping. Two words just made for each other. I told Arlene

the same thing, except one of the medium-sized buildings on the farm is gonna be my own space.

I have a huge collection of Coca-Cola collectibles and I'm gonna put them all over that place.

Walk with me and I will show you the building."

Robert was surprised to see it looked like a gas station. There were 2 antique gas pumps out front

and a sign that said, "Unleaded, 17 cents a gallon."

"Man, this outside is awesome already!" Robert exclaimed.

Cullen smiled and said, "The inside is gonna be great too! I already have the stuff for the inside!"

"Cullen, you and I are gonna have to build me one of these on my farm."

"Son, I have been collecting these things for years. I started when I was just a kid. My pawpaw

had a building that I used for storage, as I found pieces. I had a vision of what I wanted, I knew

this farm would come one day, I knew this family would come one day, I am so happy and so

excited. I can hardly wait to bring the rest of that stuff over here for my man cave. And yes, I will

help you build one for your farm!"

Reveal Day

It was only about 4 miles from Robert's farm. As they approached it, Arlene saw a double

fence and a huge wrought iron sign that said, "Arlene's Acre's"

Arlene started to cry. Cullen said, "Save them tears sweetheart. You are about to be surprised."

The house was about ¼ of an acre from the fence. "We gonna have to get Sugah a

Cart." Cullen whispered cheerfully.

"Oh, my goodness Cullen. That girl sure loved Robert Cart, didn't she? And the miracle is, she

taught herself to drive it."

The house was a farm house with a porch going all around the front, a porch swing and rocking

chairs and plants. Cullen purchased most of the furniture in the house.

Sugah rode over with Jana and Robert so she didn't hear about the golf cart or she would have

been celebrating.

Robert pulled in right behind Cullen.

Jana said, "Oh Mama, Oh Cullen, the house is beautiful."

They went inside and Arlene swooned. "Oh, my goodness Cullen. Could we afford something so

fancy? This is like in a magazine."

Cullen grabbed her and hugged her. "I want my wife to have the best. I want you to know how

happy you have made me. I want you to be comfortable for the rest of our lives Arlene."

Cullen turned and winked at Jana. She thought that was the most romantic thing anyone ever

said to her Mama.

They walked through the house, there were gorgeous hardwood floors throughout the house.

there were new kitchen appliances, a large island in the kitchen, 2 ovens, and a beautiful farm sink. A walk-in pantry for canned goods and groceries. There were 3 bedrooms downstairs and 1

bath, a laundry room complete with a new washer and dryer, and a folding table. It even had a

small sink. The living room was sunken, you had to step down 2 steps, and it had a gorgeous

chandelier.

There was a separate dining room and a breakfast room. Upstairs were 2 large bedrooms, an

additional room for a library, and 1 bathroom. The bathroom had a new soaking bathtub that

Arlene had always wanted. There were large closets. They walked outside and there was a huge

chicken coop. The barn already had 4 horses and 3 donkeys in it. There were 2 dogs, 3 cats, and

8 pygmy goats. Cullen had bought the livestock with the house.

Sugah had been quiet the entire time. She followed them down to the creek. "So, this is where

they all come get a drink?"

"If they want to Sugah, we will still give them fresh water, I don't have many rules Sugah, but I

insist you never get in the creek unless an adult is with you. It's beautiful, but it has something

called a current that can sweep you away and either hurt you or even kill you. Promise me you

won't get in it unless an adult is with you." Cullen said.

"I promise Daddy Cullen," Sugah said, putting her hand over her heart.

"Thank you Sugah. I know you always keep your word."

Sugah shook her head yes and smiled.

They continued to explore the tool buildings, Cullens Man Cave, and finally the barn.

"Jana, Sugah, I'm gonna be counting on you girls to help feed the animals. At least until you get

married."

"Sugah the barn will need to be swept occasionally and new hay and shavings put down for

the goats to sleep on. By the way, Sugah check each stall, we will wait here."

Sugah looked determined to do a good job. She said hello to each of the horses and donkeys. The

Pygmy goats were adorable and called to her for treats or food. When she reached the last stall,

she yelled, "Yeehaw!!" she came running out and asked, "Daddy Cullen is it for me? It's got a

red bow on it and my name is written on a big piece of paper. Is it really for me?"

Cullen smiled and said, "Yes, my daughter. It is for you. Try it out."

Arlene asked, "Cullen what have you done?"

"I have made one of my daughters very happy."

Sugah came flying out of the barn on her golf cart.

Arlene cried happy tears, "You are amazing Cullen. This place is amazing."

"I just want all of you to be happy and safe my dear," Cullen said as he held her for the 10$^{th}$ time

that day.

Jana and Robert held hands and smiled at her parents. It was a beautiful scene. Robert pulled

her close and kissed her forehead.

Sugah stayed in their vicinity because the land was new to her. Everyone waved as she passed

by.

Cullen said, "Welp, I guess she likes her present."

Everyone laughed. Jana said, "That is the best possible present you could have ever given

her. She loves it."

"I still have to teach her how to charge the battery. But I am sure she will pick up on it quickly."

Cullen was excited to show Arlene his man cave. "This is where my Coca-Cola collection is

gonna be on display honey."

Arlene was so happy. "Cullen it's perfect for your collection. I know it will be amazing when

you are finished."

Robert had told Jana, "Once things settle down, Cullen is going to help me build one. I've got a

big Nascar collection that I am sure you don't want me displaying in our house."

Jana laughed and said, "Yes, I think a man cave will be a great thing."

Cullen said to Arlene, "We have installed intercom systems throughout the area, so y'all can

call us from inside the house if you need anything. I will also have walkie-talkies that you and I

have access to in case one of us is too far away from the intercom system to reach."

Robert spoke up and told Jana and Arlene, "Ladies, I want to teach each of you how to shoot in

case there is ever any more trouble in our lives. I know that y'all may find this hard to accept, but

Cullen and I think it is necessary to keep y'all safe."

Jana and Arlene agreed it was the right thing to do. Cullen said, "I got one more thing to talk to

y'all about. Robert and I want to train Sugah to use something called a Stun gun."

Arlene gasped, "What? You know she is scared of guns, Cullen!"

"Yes, my love but a stun gun does not shoot bullets, Robert, you can take it from here."

Robert cleared his throat and said, "Well ladies, a stun gun does not shoot bullets. It fits in your

hand and has 2 metal prongs, er, pieces and when you pull the trigger, a small bolt of electricity

comes out. It is strong enough to make a grown man fall to the floor."

Arlene asked Robert, "Is there any way she could hurt herself?"

Robert said, no ma'am, only if she shoots herself with it. Sugah showed us how she can be

taught to do certain things, with the golf cart, and the horse. I believe with the proper training

she can do this."

Arlene looked upset, "I mean, if y'all really think it could save her in case of emergency. I mean

it seems so dangerous to me."

Robert took Arlene's hand and said, "I promise I will train with her until she understands how

and when to use it. It's for her own protection. I discussed it with our Sheriff and he allowed me

to purchase one from the department. It is a smaller version. It has a holster so she can wear it on

her belt."

Jana spoke up and said, "Mama, if I had one of these in the past, nobody would have hurt me. I

think we should try it."

Arlene finally agreed but she was still nervous. Cullen assured her it would be a wise thing to do.

Sugah pulled up on her cart and said, "Why everybody looking so serious? Am I in trouble?"

Cullen said, "No baby girl. You ain't in trouble."

The next week was busy with packing and moving. Robert took a couple of vacation days

to help Cullen with the big things.

Robert and 6 of his friends moved Cullen's belongings into the new house. Cullen

had a lot of antiques he had collected over the many years of being single. He always loved

old things and was thrilled when Arlene had said she didn't mind his collections and she too

loved antique furniture. Some were his grandmothers, some his mothers, and some he purchased

from barn sales and yard sales.

Cullen put one television in the living room and the other in Sugah's room.

He put one stereo in the living room and the other in Jana's room.

"Cullen, where did you get all of this beautiful furniture?" Arlene asked.

Cullen laughed and said, "Did you ever hear of an auction?"

Arlene said, "I don't believe I have."

Cullen said," Baby it's like this, people bring their furniture or their household wares, and the

public bids on it. They get rid of things they don't want, and buyers get what they buy.

It's fascinating to me. I have bought tools, furniture, paintings, and clocks, you will have to see

them to believe. I don't know why I bought the furniture, I just felt led to. Now I see why the

good Lord was preparing me for our lives together. I'm going to take you to some auctions one

day."

They hugged. Sugah and Jana came back. Sugah was over the moon about the TV, Cullen told her to look in her room and she squealed. Sugah was not usually affectionate, however, she ran

and hugged Cullen. He told Jana to look in her room. She came back out and hugged him and her

Mama.

The same 6 male friends of Robert's arrived at Arlene's house and helped move out the

old furniture. Arlene had put aside the things she wanted to keep. The old furniture was taken

into town and left on the curb. Strangers immediately started helping themselves to everything

that was left there. Robert spoke as he watched the old furniture being snatched up, "One man's

junk is another man's treasure."

Cullen answered, "Yep. That is absolutely true."

The furniture in the new house was gorgeous. Everyone felt like they were living in a dream.

Cullen was very happy to see all the antique furniture being used in their home. He would

enjoy telling stories about the furniture, some of which, his great-grandfather had made by

hand.

Jana's room received a new 4-post bed, a beautiful dressing table with a mirror, a hope chest,

a tall Chifforobe and a beautiful chair with a table.

Sugah's room received a TV, King king-size bed, 2 dressers, and a beautiful chair with a desk.

Arlene received a gorgeous dining room set, the table had an extra insert to make it larger and it

had 8 chairs. It was complete with a Buffet and 2 China cabinets.

"Now Cullen, you know I ain't got no dishes to put in those things. I've never even seen anything like this before" Arlene gushed.

Cullen laughed and said, "Honey, you can go shopping with the girls and pick out everything

you need to decorate the house. Think of the meals we are gonna have in this house."

They all sat down to go over the schedule for feeding the animals. Sugah spoke up, "I'm good

with all chickens. I don't mind tending to them and collecting the eggs. I just want there to be

a real good lock so they don't get away again."

Arlene smiled and said, "Yes Daddy Cullen. There has to be a real good lock." She winked at

him.

Cullen wrote down, "Real good lock on the chicken coop for Sugah."

Sugah smiled at him, and then at her mama.

They stayed to feed the animals, then went over to Robert's farm to have a piece of cake

and some coffee.

Afterward, everyone helped feed Robert's animals. Sugah rode Breezy again. Then most of the

Lancaster the family went home. Jana stayed to make dinner for Robert.

"Darling, have you decided on a date for the wedding?" Robert asked her.

"Well, this is October, so I am thinking April. Does that sound okay with you?"

Robert said, "That sounds perfect my love. Plenty of time.

"Can I ask you a question, Robert?"

"Yes honey, anything."

"Why didn't Amanda come to see me? I didn't mention it because you used that time to propose marriage to me, then Cullen and Mama got the new farm, then the move...we have all

been so busy."

Robert took her hands. "Sweetheart, Amanda has an overwhelming since of guilt about what

happened to you. She has postponed her wedding and is seeking therapy. It would be an

understatement to say she is taking it hard. I can't help her work out her feelings, so I am

the one who suggested therapy. She has been staying in Mobile with our great Aunt, Effie."

"But Robert, it was not her fault, the things that happened to me."

"I know sweetheart. Yet she feels like, since y'all planned everything together, she feels like part

of it was her fault. She also constantly thinks they would have killed her and it terrifies her."

Jana cried softly, "No Robert, I take full responsibility. We were just crazy teenagers. I acted

alone. Please tell her to not feel guilty and that I love and miss her so much."

"I will honey." He held her for a long time.

Sugah came charging in and said, "Oh my lord. Yall please save that for the honeymoon."

Robert laughed and said, "Engaged people can hug before the wedding...it's the law."

Sugah wrinkled up her nose and said," Ewww. Oh, by the way. Mama sent me over here to ask

if we will go to the hardware store for 10 curtain rods and small nails to hang pictures. She

gave me 40.00 dollars to give you."

Sugah waved the (2) 20.00 dollar bills around. Jana held out her hand and Sugah reluctantly handed over the money.

Sugah said, "Can I at least get a few apples, so Mama can make an apple pie?"

Robert said, "Absolutely Sugah. I got you covered."

Sugah smiled.

When they arrived at the hardware store, Mr. Cupra had to look in the back. He only had 8

curtain rods and needed 2 more to fill the order.

Sugah asked if she could go to the market across the street to pick out her apples. Robert spoke

up and said, "Sugah don't you want us to go too? Jana may want to pick something else out."

Jana smiled at Robert, "Yeah Sugah, I need to see if he has any pumpkins for our porches and

Some winter squash sounds good. Don't it?"

Sugah looked a little disappointed, but finally said, "Yeah, I guess."

Robert and Cullen had told everyone, "There is safety in numbers ladies. Yall stick together

when you go anywhere."

Mr. Cupra came back with the 2 missing rods and the small nails.

After Robert paid for the order, Mr. Cupra said, "I just want to congratulate you two on your

engagement."

Robert and Jana both smiled big and said, "Thank you, sir."

Sugah spoke up and said, "Hey Mr. Cupra, did you know it is okay to hug if you are engaged?

Yuck!"

Jana shut her eyes and shook her head. Anything was liable to come out of that child's mouth.

Robert and Mr. Cupra laughed.

"The weddings gonna be in April, Mr. Cupra. You and the misses are welcome. We will have a big outdoor reception afterward. My friend, Austin, has a band and they will be playing on the

church grounds. We sure hope y'all will come."

"I wouldn't miss it, Robert. I have watched you and these 2 girls grow up." Mr. Cupra said

Smiling

Sugah rolled her eyes and said, "Yeah, he told Mama to keep me out of here, but you

gonna invite him to your wedding. That's just stupid. I'm gonna wait out front for y'all."

She stormed off.

Mr. Cupra looked embarrassed and said, "There are just some strange men who might not

be kind to Sugah. I wasn't doing it to be mean."

Jana said, "It's okay Mr. Cupra. Not everyone understands Sugah."

Sugah was angry and she paced back and forth, cussing to herself. How could Jana be

so stupid to invite him. They probably invited that old hag from the glass shop too.

A man called to her, "Hey Sugah, come over here. Do you know where the post office is?"

She yelled back, "Go down the street a little bit more and it's on this side." She was

pointing to her left.

"Do you remember me?" he called back to her. "Why don't you come here so we can stop

yelling at each other? I wanna talk to you?"

Sugah walked over to him, still mad.

"Where do I know ya from?" Sugah asked.

"I used to work at the hardware store you just came outta."

"Oh yeah? That old man is a jerk."

"You're telling me. He fired me because I forgot to come to work one day. Anyhow can

you come look at this puppy I got in the truck? I think it might be sick. Tell me what you think."

"Well, I ain't no doctor but I will look at it."

He walked over behind the market, "I parked back here."

Sugah walked over to his truck, but when they got back there, he grabbed her and tried

to put a burlap sack over her head. He didn't count on Sugah fighting and screaming like she

did. He tore her shirt open, trying to hold on to her. She scratched his face and kicked out his

passenger-side window. He punched her in the side of the face as she got away. Sugah ran back

to Robert and Jana for help. It took her a few seconds to explain what had happened. She was

crying and shaking violently.

Robert jumped in his truck and tore down the road trying to find the gray truck that

Sugah had described. The man got away. Mr. Cupra had called for the doctor to come check

Sugah and Jana had called for Arlene to come into town. Jana didn't tell Arlene what

happened, she just asked her to come pick them up because Robert had to leave. By the time

Arlene arrived and saw Sugah's face was swollen, her lip busted and her nose had been

bleeding. Arlene was shocked, Sugah had breasts and they were showing through her torn t-shirt.

Arlene had not noticed that before and it unnerved her.

All of this was just too much. Sugah was so innocent. Arlene thought, "Why would anyone do this to my baby."

She tried to be brave and not cry in front of Sugah and Jana. But inside her heart was crushed.

The doctor arrived and examined Sugah, however, he asked Arlene to inquire if the man had

touched her inappropriately. Sugah said, "No mama. And I didn't see no puppy either."

Arlene asked the doctor to have a look at Jana and make sure she was okay. The doctor

spoke to Jana. Arlene heard Jana crying. The doctor came back and gave Arlene medication for

both girls for anxiety.

Robert came back. He had no luck finding the truck or the man. He called the Sheriff to let

him know what happened. The sheriff said to try and get a better description of the man and

the truck from Sugah, once she calmed down.

Jana was stricken with grief. She knew it was somebody from her past trying to make her pay for

escaping.

The Sheriff's department had something called a BOLO (Be on the Lookout) that was sent to

surrounding counties and to everyone's relief, the man in that truck was stopped and arrested as

soon as he crossed over the county line.

Robert took everyone home to Arlene and Cullen's house. When Cullen arrived, he was angry.

The kind of angry, that would make a man kill someone. Robert called the family to the jail in

Watson County to see if Jana or Sugah could identify the man.

It was only a 30-minute drive to the Watson County Jail. The man was put into a line-up. There was a 2 way mirror that the women could see the men but the men couldn't see them. There

were 6 men standing in the lineup.

Sugah and Jana did not know that 5 of those men were police officers and deputy sheriffs. There

was only one man that was a bad guy.

As soon as Sugah walked it, before any instruction had been given to her.

She blurted out, "It's number 3. That is the man who jumped on me and punched me in my face

and put a bag over my head. You see his black eye? I got one good lick in. You don't mess with

Cullen and Arlene's children or you'll get your ass kicked."

Arlene instinctively pulled Sugah away from the window. Jana stepped up to the window and

said, "That man, number 3, he works with the people who kidnapped me. I heard someone call

him Cholly. Once I called him Charlie and he stopped me and said, "It's Cholly, C H O L L Y.

He spelled it out, then he hit me in the head and told me, "Don't tell nobody I told you, my

name. The boss don't let us use our names in this here operation."

Arlene asked if they could leave since the man had been identified. The Sheriff said yes.

Cullen drove the girls home. Robert stayed behind with his Sheriff to watch the interview.

Cholly started spilling names, addresses, and victims when given incentives. He said he was

promised five hundred dollars to kidnap Sugah, Jana's retarded sister, as payback to Jana for

running away from Raymond Johnson. He gave Raymond Johnson's address, and information as to where he was to deliver Sugah and where he was to pick up his money. Robert's Sheriff told him to ride with him and they would go arrest Raymond Johnson. "I have a feeling he is going to resist so you better come with me. I believe we can deliver a message to him from Jana and Sugah."

As it was Raymond Johnson did resist. He used his last 22 bullets for a shoot-out, and then the officers charged into the house to apprehend him. He and Robert had about 5 minutes of hand-to-hand combat, where Robert administered a good old-fashioned beating to him. When the sheriff thought he had enough he pulled Robert off of him and handcuffed him. "Thank God you were here Robert. I thought he was gonna get away." The sheriff joked.

Raymond was taken into custody and charged with everything in the book. He was given 5 life sentences. He gave names, dates, addresses, and telephone numbers, and still was not given a deal. He would never get out of prison. 25 people were arrested from the information he provided. None of them were given deals either.

Jana and Sugah could finally feel safe. Arlene, Cullen, and Robert could finally rest easy that their girls would be okay.

*

# Also by Lilly Buchanan

**Bad girls**
Jezebel
Rahab

**King Marc 1**
King Marc

**Life in a small town**
New Life in a Small Town

**Standalone**
Class B Dependent
Our Second Chance
Dannie
Leroy
Sugah

# About the Author

Lilly Buchanan is originally from Columbus, Georgia. She currently lives in Pascagoula, Mississippi. Lilly started writing when she was a little girl. Lilly loves pretty things, flowers, decorating, writing beautiful stories, volunteering and Jesus! Lilly has 2 amazing granddaughters, Jasmine and Alexandria. If you stop and ask she will show you pictures!!